Giants! My bedtime stories were full of them.
My mother, Barbara, told me tales of giants, fierce and
tall as mountains. We would shiver under the covers
together, just thinking of them. But Barbara and I would
always trick them in the end – before the lights went off!
Here are two of our most fearsome giants…and a dose
of wicked bandits, too!

ANNA FIENBERG

Anna and Barbara Fienberg write the Tashi stories together,
making up all kinds of daredevil adventures and tricky
characters for him to face. Lucky he's such a clever Tashi.

Kim Gamble is one of Australia's favourite illustrators
for children. Together Kim and Anna have made such
wonderful books as *The Magnificent Nose and Other*
Marvels, *The Hottest Boy Who Ever Lived*, the *Tashi* series,
the *Minton* picture books, *Joseph,* and a full colour picture
book about their favourite adventurer, *There once was*
a boy called Tashi.

D0956449

Anna Fienberg would like to thank the Literature Board of the Australia Council for their assistance.

First published in 1995
This edition first published in 2006

Copyright © Text, Anna Fienberg and Barbara Fienberg, 1995
Copyright © Illustrations, Kim Gamble, 1995

All rights reserved. No part of this book may be reproduced or transmitted in any form or by any means, electronic or mechanical, including photocopying, recording or by any information storage and retrieval system, without prior permission in writing from the publisher. The *Australian Copyright Act 1968* (the Act) allows a maximum of one chapter or ten per cent of this book, whichever is the greater, to be photo-copied by any educational institution for its educational purposes provided that the educational institution (or body that administers it) has given a remuneration notice to Copyright Agency Limited (CAL) under the Act.

Allen & Unwin
83 Alexander St
Crows Nest NSW 2065
Australia
Phone: (61 2) 8425 0100
Fax: (61 2) 9906 2218
Email: info@allenandunwin.com
Web: www.allenandunwin.com

National Library of Australia
Cataloguing-in-Publication entry:

Fienberg, Anna.
  Tashi and the giants.

  New cover ed.
  For primary school children.
  ISBN 978 1 74114 966 1.

  ISBN 1 74114 966 5.

  1. Children's stories, Australian. 2. Tashi (Fictitious character) – Juvenile fiction. I. Fienberg, Barbara. II. Gamble, Kim. III. Title. (Series: Tashi; 2).

A823.3

Cover and series design by Sandra Nobes
Typeset in Sabon by P.I.X.E.L. Pty Ltd, Melbourne
Printed in Australia by McPhersons Printing Group

10 9 8 7 6 5 4 3 2

Tashi

and the
GIANTS

written by
**Anna
Fienberg**

and

**Barbara
Fienberg**

•

illustrated by
Kim Gamble

ALLEN&UNWIN

Jack ran all the way to school on Tuesday morning. He was so early, the streets were empty. Good. That meant he would have plenty of time to hear Tashi's new story.

5

Tashi was Jack's new friend. He'd come from a land far away, where he'd met fire-breathing dragons and fearsome warlords. Today, Tashi had promised the story of Chintu, the giant.

Tashi was waiting for Jack on a seat by the cricket pitch.

'So,' said Jack, when he'd stopped puffing and they were sitting comfortably. 'Did you really meet a giant, Tashi?'

'Yes,' said Tashi. 'It was like this. Do you remember how I tricked the dragon, and put out his fire? Well, the dragon was furious, and he flew to the castle where his friend Chintu the giant lived. The dragon told him what I had done and Chintu boomed:

"Fee fie fo fum

I'll catch that boy for you, by gum!"

'Chintu took one of his giant steps over to our village and hurled down great boulders, just as if they were bowling balls. Third Uncle's house was squashed flat as a fritter. Then the giant roared, "Bring Tashi out to me."

'The giant looked terrible standing there, so tall
he cast a shadow over the whole village. He was
as big as a mountain—imagine, a mountain that
moved!—and tufts of hair stood up on his head
like spiky trees.'

'So what did you do?' Jack shuddered.

'Well, it was like this. My father, who is a very
brave man, ran out into the street and cried,
"Be gone, Chintu, we will never give Tashi up
to you!"

'The giant was quiet for a moment. Then he
answered, "If you don't bring Tashi to me, I
will come back in the morning and crush every
house in the village."

11

'The people all gathered in the square to discuss what to do. Some wanted to take me to the giant's house that night. Others were braver and said I should run away. While they were still arguing, I took the lantern and set out for Chintu's castle.

'I walked and walked until finally, there before me was the giant's castle, towering up to the sky. One path led up to a great door and windows filled with light, but another led down some winding stone steps.

'I took the lower path but the steps were so high I had to jump from each one as if they were small cliffs. After a while I spied an arched wooden door. It wasn't locked and I pushed it open. It gave a groaning creak and a voice called out, "Who's there? Is that you, Chintu, you fly-bitten lump of cowardly husband?"

'Now I saw a big stone-floored room and right

in the middle was an enormous cage. Inside the cage was another giant.'

'Ooh!' said Jack. 'Two giants! Didn't you want
to run?'
'No,' said Tashi. 'Not me. See, it was like this.
The giant in the cage was sitting at a table
eating some noodles. She was terrible to look
at. She had only four teeth, yellow as sandstone,
and the gaps in between were as big as caves.

'Well, while I was staring at her she said in a huge voice, "Who are you?"

'So I told her that I was Tashi and what had happened and that I had come to persuade Chintu not to kill me. She gave a laugh like thunder and said, "You won't change his mind easily, it sets like concrete. I should know, he is my husband! He tricked me into this cage and locked me up, all because we had an argument about the best way to make dumplings. He likes to grind bones for them, but I say flour is much better. Now Tashi, you need me to help you."'

16

'And she needed you to help *her*!' Jack said
excitedly.

'Right,' said Tashi. 'So when she pointed to the
keys over on a stool, I reached up and dragged
them over to her. Mrs Chintu snatched them
up and turned one in the lock. "Now I'll show
that lumbering worms-for-brains Chintu who
is the cleverer of us two!"

'As she walked past, I scrambled up her skirts and hung on to her belt. She picked up a mighty club that was standing by the door and then she tip-toed to some stairs that led up and up through the middle of the castle.

'We came to a vast hall and there he was,
sitting on a bench like a mountain bent in the
middle. He was staring into the fire, bellowing
a horrible song:

"Fee fie fo foy,

   Tomorrow I'll go and get that boy,

   No matter if he's dead or jumping

   I'll grind his bones to make my dumpling."

'Mrs Chintu crept up behind him, grabbed his tufty hair in one hand and held up the club with the other. I slid down her back to the floor.

'"Chintu, you pig-headed grump of a husband, I can escape from your cages, *and* I make the best dumplings. Will you admit now that I am more than a match for you?"

'The giant rolled his great eyes and caught sight of me. "Who is that?" he roared.

'"That is the boy who chops our wood." And Mrs Chintu winked at me. "Now, let the boy decide who makes the best dumplings." She let go of Chintu's hair and gave me a hard look.
'"Very well," Chintu said, and he rubbed his huge hands together.

'Later, they put some sacks down on the floor for me to sleep on. As he was going to bed, Chintu whispered—it was like a thunderclap in my ear—"If you decide that *her* dumplings are better, your bones will make my next batch."

And as his wife went by, she said, "If you decide that *his* dumplings are better, I'll chop you up for my next pot of soup."

'All night I walked up and down the stone
floor, thinking what to do. And then I had one
of my cunning ideas. I crept downstairs to the
kitchen and had a good look about.'

'What were you looking for, Tashi?' asked Jack.

'Well,' said Tashi, 'it was like this. The next morning Mrs Chintu boiled her dumplings and then Chintu boiled his. When the dumplings were cooked they both spooned up one each, as big as footballs.

'"We must put a blindfold on the boy so he doesn't know which dumpling he is eating," said Mrs Chintu, and her husband tied a handkerchief over my eyes.

'I took a bite of one dumpling and swallowed it slowly. Then I tried the other. They watched me fiercely.

'When I had finished I said, "These are the best dumplings I ever tasted, and they are exactly the same."

'"No they're not!" thundered Chintu.

'"Taste them yourself and see," I said.

'So they did and they were very surprised.
"The boy is right. They *are* the same," said
Mrs Chintu. "And they are the best dumplings
I ever tasted."

'So then I told them, "That's because I went
downstairs to the kitchen last night and I
mixed the ground bones and the flour together.
That's what makes the best dumplings—bones
and flour."

'"What a clever Tashi," cried Mrs Chintu.

'"Oho! So that's who you are," bellowed Chintu, and he scooped me up in his great red hands. "I promised my friend the dragon that I would serve you up to him in a tasty fritter the next time he came to breakfast."

'"Maybe so," said his wife, "but just try another dumpling first."

'The giant did, and when he had finished he thought for a minute. It was the longest minute of my life. Then the giant sighed and licked his lips. "Dragon can have a plate of these dumplings instead," he said. "They are exquisite. Be off with you now, Tashi."

'And so this time I walked out the great front door, as bold as you please. When I returned to the village they were still arguing about whether to give me up to Chintu or to let me run away. "I don't have to do either!" I cried, and I told them what had happened.

'"What a clever Tashi!" cried Grandmother.'

'So that's the end of the story,' said Jack sadly. 'And everyone was safe and happy again.'

'Yes,' said Tashi, 'that is, until the bandits arrived.'

THE BANDITS

One night Jack was reading a book with his father.

'This story reminds me of the time Tashi was captured by some bandits,' said Jack.

'Oh good, another Tashi story,' said Dad. 'I suppose Tashi finished up as the Bandit Chief.' 'No, he didn't,' said Jack. 'It was like this. One wet and windy night a band of robbers rode into Tashi's village. They were looking for some shelter for the night.

'But next morning, just as they were leaving, the wife of the Bandit Chief saw Tashi. He reminded her of her son, who had sailed away on a pirate ship, and she said to her husband, "That boy looks just like our son, Mo Chi. Let's take him with us."

'So Tashi was picked up and thrown on to one
of the horses and away they went. He sneaked
a good look about him, but he was surrounded
by bandits, and it was impossible to escape. So
Tashi had to think up one of his cunning plans.

'The first night when the bandits were still
sitting around the fire after their dinner, the
Bandit Chief said to Tashi, "Come, boy, sing us
a song as Mo Chi did, of treasure and pirates
and fish that shine like coins in the sea."

'Tashi saw that this was his chance. So what do you think he did?'

'Sang like a nightingale,' said Dad.
'Wrong!' said Jack. 'He sang like a crow. The bandits all covered their ears and the Bandit Wife said, "Stop, stop! You sing like a crow.

You had better come over here and brush my hair like my son used to do." Tashi bowed politely but as he stepped around the fire, he filled the brush with thistles and burrs so that soon her hair was full of tangles.

'"Stop, stop!" cried the Bandit Wife, and her husband told her, "This boy is not like our son. He sings like a crow and he tangles your hair." Tashi put on a sorrowful face. "I will do better tomorrow," he promised.

'"You'd better," whispered the Chief's brother, Me Too, "or I'll boil you in snake oil."

'The next day when the bandits moved camp,
they put all the rice into three big bags and
gave them to Tashi to carry. When they came
to a river, what do you think Tashi did?'

'Well,' said Dad, scratching his chin, 'he's such
a clever boy, I expect he carried them over one
by one, holding them up high.'

'Wrong!' said Jack. 'He dropped them all into the river. The bandits roared with rage. They called to Tashi to mind the horses. Then they jumped into the water and tried to recover the bags of rice that were sinking further down the river.'

'But Tashi reached them first, I suppose,'
said Dad.

'No, he didn't,' said Jack, 'and when the
bandits came back, all angry and dripping,
they found that he had lost all the horses. The
robbers began to whisper about the Bandit
Wife, and Me Too gave Tashi evil looks. It
took them a whole day to find the horses
again.

'Well, that night, the Bandit Chief said to his wife, "This boy is not like our son. He sings like a crow, he tangles your hair, he loses the rice and scatters the horses." Tashi put on a sorrowful face. "I will do better tomorrow," he promised.

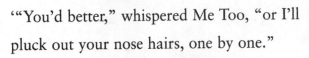

'"You'd better," whispered Me Too, "or I'll pluck out your nose hairs, one by one."

'On the third day, the bandits decided to attack
the village where another band of robbers were
staying. Just before dawn they quietly
surrounded the camp—and what do you think
Tashi did then?'

'He rode into the village and captured the
chief,' guessed Dad.

'Wrong!' cried Jack. 'They were just preparing
to attack, when Tashi accidentally let off his
gun.

'The enemy was warned and Tashi's bandits
had to gallop away for their lives.

When they were at a safe distance they stopped. The Chief's brother wanted to punish Tashi—he said he'd tie him up and smother him in honey and let man-eating ants loose upon him—but the Bandit Wife said, "No, let him come back to camp with me. He can help me roast the ducks we stole yesterday and we will have a feast ready for you when you return."

'So she and Tashi worked all day, plucking, chopping and turning the ducks on the spit, and mouth-watering smells greeted the bandits as they drew near the camp that evening. And what do you think Tashi did then?'

'Washed his hands for dinner,' said Dad.

'Wrong!' said Jack. 'Just as the robbers jumped
down from their horses, Tashi stumbled and
knocked a big pot of cold water over the
almost-cooked ducks and put out the fire.

'"Enough!" shouted the Bandit Chief to his wife. "This boy is not like our son. He sings like a crow, he tangles your hair, he loses the rice, he scatters the horses, he warns our enemies—and now he has spoilt our dinner. This is too much." And he turned to Tashi.

"You must go home to your village now,
Tashi. You are a clumsy, useless boy with no
more brain than the ducks you ruined."

'Tashi smiled inside, but he put on a sorrowful
face and turned to the Bandit Wife. "I'm sorry
that I wasn't like your son," he said, but she
was already on her way down to the river to
fetch some more water.

'Tashi turned to go when a rough hand pulled him back.

'"You don't deserve to go free, Duck Spoiler," snarled Me Too. "Say goodbye to this world and hullo to the next because I'm going to make an end of you."

'But as he turned to pick up his deadly nose-hair plucker, Tashi shook himself free and tore off into the forest. He could hear the bandit crashing through the trees after him, but if he could just make it to the river, he thought he would have a chance.

'He was almost there when he heard a splash. He looked up to see the Bandit Wife had slipped on a stone and had fallen into the water.

'"Help!" she cried when she saw Tashi. "Help me, I can't swim!"

'Tashi hesitated. He could ignore her, and dive in and swim away. But he couldn't leave her to drown, even though she was a bandit. So he swam over to her and pulled her ashore.

'By now all the bandits were lined up along
the bank and the Chief ran up to Tashi.
"Thank you, Tashi. I take back all those hard
words I said about you. Fate did send you to
us after all."

'Me Too groaned and gnashed his teeth.

'"Brother," said the Bandit Chief, "you can see Tashi safely home."

'"Oh no, thanks," said Tashi quickly, "I know the way," and he nipped off up the bank of the river, quicker than the wind.'

'So,' said Dad sadly, 'that's the end of the story and Tashi arrived safely back at his village.'

'Wrong!' said Jack. 'He did arrive back at the village and there were great celebrations. But at the end of the night, when everyone was going sleepily to bed, Third Uncle noticed that a ghost-light was shining in the forest.'

'And that's another Tashi story, I'll bet!'
cried Dad.

'Right!' said Jack. 'But we'll save it for dinner
when Mum gets home.'